...ible
world of the Night Zoo

Me... ...ing
magical creatures!

Follow Will's adventure
as he becomes the
Night Zookeeper

Beware of the evil
army of Voids

Continue to explore
the Night Zoo at
nightzookeeper.com

Meet the Characters

Will

The new Night Zookeeper, a force for good in a magical world that's under threat from an evil army of darkness.

Grandma

Loves adventuring to faraway places and always returns with plenty of stories to tell.

Riya

Fast, brave, impulsive. She never lets a silly thing like rules stand in her way.

Sam

Extremely tall and extremely clumsy, but when it comes to spying, he's the best.

The Voids

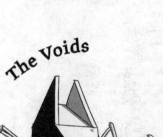

Robotic spiders set on destroying the Night Zoo and plunging it into darkness.

This book was co-written by Giles Clare

OXFORD
UNIVERSITY PRESS

Great Clarendon Street, Oxford OX2 6DP

Oxford University Press is a department of the University of Oxford.
It furthers the University's objective of excellence in research, scholarship,
and education by publishing worldwide. Oxford is a registered trade mark of
Oxford University Press in the UK and in certain other countries

British Library Cataloguing in Publication Data

Data available

ISBN: 978-0-19-276405-8

1 3 5 7 9 10 8 6 4 2

Printed in Great Britain

Paper used in the production of this book is a natural,
recyclable product made from wood grown in sustainable forests.
The manufacturing process conforms to the environmental
regulations of the country of origin.

NIGHT ZOO KEEPER

The Giraffes of Whispering Wood

Joshua Davidson

Illustrated by Buzz Burman

OXFORD
UNIVERSITY PRESS

Chapter One

Will Rivers took a step back from the wall. He clamped the end of his paintbrush between his teeth and admired his work. Well, his painting was certainly big. And purple. Very purple. Will smiled with satisfaction. He had captured the shape and features really well. It looked great. Almost perfect in fact.

A voice next to him said, 'Oh mate, what have you done?'

Will hadn't noticed his friend Isaac come and stand next to him. Isaac was examining Will's painting with a sour look on his face.

'I mean, seriously. That's not how an elephant should look,' said Isaac.

'What d'you mean?' replied Will.

'Durr! The colour. What's that about?'

'What's wrong with it?' asked Will.

'What are you? Six?' said Isaac. 'Make-believe stuff is fine for sad little kids in the infants who don't know anything. Now it's just tragic.'

Will felt his cheeks glowing warmly. Not for the first time, he wondered why he was friends with Isaac.

Isaac continued, 'The teacher is not going to be happy with you; everyone else is doing it right. Look.'

Isaac pointed to the line of children stretched out along the wall of the zoo. Will looked at his classmates, who were all busy painting different animals on the wall. His new teacher, Mrs Barnes, was inspecting a tiger painted by a group of girls. It was Mrs Barnes who had organized this whole special project to paint a giant mural on the wall of the local zoo. She had reminded the class several times what an honour it was. She had also reminded them not to mess it up. Many times. Will frowned.

'Seriously, mate. Why couldn't you just do a

normal elephant?' asked Isaac with a sigh.

'I was being creative,' muttered Will.

'Well, you weren't told to do that. It's probably against the rules.'

Will gulped. 'Rules? What rules?' He glanced over at Mrs Barnes nervously.

'Durr! The rules of life. You know? Elephants are grey, zebras are black and white, penguins are orange.'

'Orange?' repeated Will.

Isaac rolled his eyes. 'I was being sarcastic.'

Will looked at his giant picture of the purple elephant. He suddenly realized what was missing.

'Anyway, it isn't finished yet,' he told Isaac firmly. He picked up a clean paintbrush and grabbed a tube of bright yellow paint. He squeezed a blob onto his palette. Will stepped forward and painted a large yellow symbol in the centre of the elephant's forehead.

'Oh, very realistic,' said Isaac with a slow shake of his head. 'What's that?'

'An eternity symbol,' replied Will. 'It's the same as the tattoo my grandma got in India.'

'Your grandma's got a tattoo?' said Isaac, wrinkling up his nose.

'Yeah! She's got loads. So what?' said Will.

'You're gonna be in such trouble for this,' Isaac muttered and sloped off back to his place in the line.

Will tried to pretend he didn't care. He spotted Mrs Barnes wandering in his direction and his heart suddenly raced in his chest. Will didn't want to get in trouble. He never set out to break the rules. He was the only person in his family who was normal like that.

'Pack up your things, Year Five,' called out Mrs Barnes. 'Time to walk back to school.'

Will sighed with relief. He quickly packed up his materials. As he headed off to join his class, he glanced back at his purple painting. Although he was still worried about being in trouble, he really liked it. There was something kind of magical about it and he was proud of himself.

Will flung open the back gate to his house. He stalked down the side of the strange shed that his grandma lived in at the bottom of the garden. Ahead of him, Will could hear his grandma's voice. She spoke with such a big, rich voice for such a tiny person. She was telling one of her stories. 'And just in time, the Ant General ordered the army of ants to help,' she was saying.

Will entered the garden and saw his grandma sitting on the steps of her shed.

Across from her, Will's six-year-old brother Charlie was lying on the grass with his head on his scrunched-up school jumper. Their grandma, with her wild white hair and battered walking boots, peered over her glasses at Will. 'Good afternoon,' she said.

'Hi, Grandma,' Will replied quietly. He kept walking. He wasn't in the mood to chat. Will's pride in his painting had worn off. He had been fretting on his walk home. Isaac had been right. Why had he done it purple?

Elephants were grey. That was how you were supposed to paint them. He was going to be in trouble for sure.

'Join us for the story?' asked his grandma. Will pretended not to hear her and continued towards the house. 'Will, dear, is everything okay?' she asked.

'Sorry, Grandma,' he replied over his shoulder. 'I've got tons of homework to do. Mrs Barnes, our new teacher, gives us loads extra.'

'Hey, Will,' said Charlie. 'Wait a sec.'

Will turned towards him. His scruffy little brother was smiling at him. 'What?' Will said impatiently.

'I've got a new teacher too.'

'No you haven't.'

'I have! She's got wonky eyes,' insisted Charlie.

'No, Charlie. Not one of your jokes, please,' groaned Will.

'I'm not joking. She's a rubbish teacher though.'

'Why?'

'She can't control her pupils!' Charlie said and giggled. 'Geddit?'

'Oh, Charlie, I love it!' exclaimed Grandma Rivers. She threw her head back and honked with laughter. Will smiled weakly and turned towards the house. Grandma Rivers lifted her glasses and wiped away a tear. 'Right, where were we?' she said. 'Ahhh yes, and as everyone knows, an army of ants can be as strong as an ox.' And with that, she continued her story.

'Ants aren't like oxen and elephants aren't purple,' Will muttered to himself. 'Stupid make-believe, stupid jokes, stupid mural.'

'Hi, Will,' said a girl's voice. It was Riya, Will's next-door neighbour. He hadn't noticed her before as she was sitting on top of the wall between their houses. Will looked up at his friend. He wasn't sure he would be quite so confident up that high. 'Oh, hi,' he replied. 'Your hair. You've changed it again. It looks kind of purple. And silver.'

Riya smiled and nodded. 'I couldn't decide, so I just went for both,' she said with  a shrug. 'Mum's cross about it. Says I never think things through.'

'Looks cool,' said Will.

'I've got some of the purple spray left. You want it?' she asked.

Will shook his head quickly. 'Come on, Will. Where's your sense of adventure?' Riya asked with a smirk. Will looked away. He wouldn't have dared to dye his hair, especially without permission. Riya changed the subject. 'Well, are you both excited?' she asked. 'You and Grandma Rivers? It's both your birthdays tomorrow. You're going to catch up with me at last, right?'

Will felt his cheeks glow a little: Riya was nearly eleven. 'Sure, ten. Tomorrow,' he said.

A cross voice called out from next door's garden, 'Riya, I've told you before. Get down from there. It's dangerous!'

Riya twisted round. 'But I'm listening to Grandma Rivers' story,' she protested.

'Get down and come and tidy up this mess you've made please,' replied Riya's mum.

Riya turned back to Will. 'Well, happy birthday for tomorrow,' she said and swung her legs back over the wall. 'See ya.' She dropped out of sight, but seconds later, Will heard her talking to her mum.

'It's not a mess. It's a sculpture,' Riya said.

'Made from my onions and potatoes?' exclaimed her mum.

Will smiled. 'See ya,' he said and headed up the steps to the back door.

That night, Will couldn't get to sleep. On the bunk bed below, Charlie had gone out like a light and was snoring loudly. Will wondered what present his parents had bought him. Please let it be the phone, he thought. He was going to be ten after all. Ten! He wondered if he'd feel different in the morning. More grown-up and clever, like Riya. Charlie's snoring was getting even louder. Will huffed. A phone would be great, he thought, but so would having his own room.

There was another noise in the distance.

Will recognized it. The zoo was only a few streets away and Will could often hear the animals. He realized the window was open and the sound of squawking flamingos was drifting in on the night air.

Will climbed down the ladder and crossed over to the window. He opened a chink in the curtain and peered out over the rooftops in the direction of the zoo. The flamingos were still screeching and squawking. Will wondered why they were being so noisy. He yanked the window shut to muffle the noise. As he did so, he knocked into one of his pot plants on the windowsill.

He caught it just as it tipped over the edge. He let out a low whistle of relief: it was his favourite Venus flytrap. Will examined its purple clam-shaped leaves with their long green teeth for any signs of damage. He then replaced the pot carefully on the sill. Out of the corner of his eye, he caught sight of a figure in the garden below. It was his grandma. She was standing still in the middle of the lawn in her nightie. Her wild white hair was glowing in the moonlight. She had her back to him, her head tilted to one side. What was she doing? She's listening, thought Will.

Listening to those flamingos. In her nightie.

'You're so weird, Grandma,' he said under his breath, and returned to bed.

Chapter Two

'**H**ello Will, my dear. Have you finished?'

Will turned to see Grandma Rivers peering over his shoulder at his painting.

'Grandma, what are you doing here?' he asked in surprise.

'Oh, I was just passing and spotted you.' She was examining the purple elephant carefully. 'It's wonderful,' she said. 'The eternity symbol is perfect.'

'Thanks,' said Will.

'And these magnificent gates? Did you do those too?'

'No,' replied Will looking at the painting of some tall gates next to his elephant. 'That was someone else.'

'Well, anyway, your painting is perfect. You couldn't have given me a better present,' said Grandma Rivers, beaming.

Will wasn't sure what she meant. His painting was part of his class project, not a present for Grandma Rivers. He was about to correct her when he remembered what her actual present was. He had wrapped it in a rush before school: a pair of woolly bedsocks. He felt a twinge of guilt as he remembered he hadn't even bought the socks himself: his mum had picked them up for him.

'I'm glad you like it, Grandma,' he said.

'I'm not sure *I* do,' said a voice.

Will turned to see his teacher Mrs Barnes examining his painting. She wrinkled her nose and tutted three times in quick succession. Isaac was lurking next to her, his hands behind his back. He smiled smugly at Will. Will clenched his jaw. It was obvious that Isaac had told their teacher about his purple picture. Now Isaac was hanging about desperately hoping to see Will get into trouble.

'Oh dear,' said Mrs Barnes. 'What a pity.

Not exactly what I was looking for, zoologically-speaking.'

Isaac sniggered. Will flushed with a mix of embarrassment and irritation.

'Does it matter?' asked Grandma Rivers.

Mrs Barnes gave Grandma Rivers a questioning look. 'Well, I've never seen a purple elephant, have you?'

'You'd be surprised,' replied Will's grandma.

'And what's that thing on its forehead?' Mrs Barnes asked.

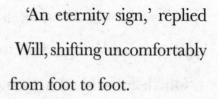

'An eternity sign,' replied Will, shifting uncomfortably from foot to foot.

'Where did you get that silly idea from?' she exclaimed.

'Right here,' said Grandma Rivers firmly. She rolled up the sleeve of her cardigan. Mrs Barnes almost gasped in surprise as she caught sight of the eternity tattoo on Grandma Rivers' forearm.

'Oh, how unusual,' said Mrs Barnes.

Will's chest suddenly throbbed with pride for his grandma.

'Would you like to see some of my other ones?' asked Grandma Rivers. She glanced at Will. Her eyes were twinkling behind her round spectacles. Will's mouth dropped open in horror as he realized what she was about to do.

'Grandma, not those tattoos,' he pleaded quietly.

She winked at him and turned back to Mrs Barnes. 'I've got a big tattoo right here.' She lifted up the bottom of her cardigan and hooked a thumb into the elastic waistband of her long skirt. She began to pull the top of her skirt down towards her bottom. Mrs Barnes looked alarmed and Isaac put his hands over his eyes.

'Please stop right there,' Mrs Barnes interrupted quickly. 'Think of the children!'

Grandma Rivers removed her thumb and smiled sweetly at the teacher. Will, who had been holding his breath, sighed with relief.

Mrs Barnes recovered herself. 'I'm sorry, Will, I must insist,' she said. 'You need to change your picture.'

'What?' said Will. 'No, please.'

Mrs Barnes ignored him. 'Isaac,' she said. 'The paint please.' Isaac stepped forward with a grin, revealing what he had been hiding behind his back: a large pot of thick, grey paint and a gunky paintbrush.

Will's heart sank. Mrs Barnes held out the brush towards him. Will turned to Grandma Rivers for help. To his surprise, Grandma Rivers pulled him into a powerful hug and whispered in his ear. 'Remember, that elephant can be anything you want it to be. All you need to do is believe. You're ready. You're finally ready!' She released him and smiled brightly. 'Anyway, I'm off! Gotta see a man about a crocodile,' she announced. 'Goodbye, Mrs Boring! Whoops, I mean Barnes. Boring Barnes! Silly me!' Mrs Barnes scowled. Will covered his mouth to hide his smile. And without another word, Grandma Rivers strode away on her short, sturdy legs.

Mrs Barnes fixed Will with a stern look. 'You know what to do, young man,' she said. Reluctantly, Will took the brush and pot of paint. Mrs Barnes turned on her heel and stalked away. Isaac scurried after her. Will turned to see Grandma Rivers disappearing around the corner of the street. He laughed.

She had been so rude, threatening to show her tattooed bottom and calling his teacher Mrs Boring! Will stared at the brush in his hand and then at his picture. He shook his head and then started work. As he covered over the purple paint with the grey, his grandma's words echoed in his mind: 'You're ready. You're finally ready!' Will shook his head. Ready for what, he wondered. His grandma really was strange.

After school, Will was sitting at the kitchen table. His mum had made a huge, wonky cake. Each layer was a different, bright colour and it was decorated with sprinkles, bonbons, and candied fruit.

'I helped,' said his brother proudly.

'No kidding,' replied Will.

He thought that next year he might ask for a plain cake from the supermarket. 'Where's Grandma?' he asked. 'And where's her cake?'

'I'll get her,' announced Charlie.

'Hang on, Charlie,' said Will's mum quickly. Will saw her swap a look with his dad.

'The thing is . . . well, she's gone away.'

'You mean, she's not here?' asked Will.

'Sorry, Will, I just went to check. Her shed's all locked up,' said his dad. 'She only told us she was going away this morning. She's off on one of her adventures. You know what she's like.'

Will felt a bit hollow inside. It was the first time he could remember his grandma not being there. They had always celebrated their birthdays together. Couldn't she have waited one day? It didn't feel the same. There would be no amazing story this year. There would be fewer candles and fewer laughs.

'But I haven't given her my present,' he said.

'It's okay,' said his mum. 'I gave it to her before she left. And she left you this.' Will's mum handed him a round package. It felt heavy for its size. Will removed and read the gift tag:

From Here Begins The Battle

Will peeled the wrapping paper apart and looked at the object inside: it was a large glass sphere, like an oversized paperweight. The glass was cloudy.

'What's she given you this time?' his dad asked.

'No idea,' Will replied. He examined the sphere more closely. He had been wrong.

It wasn't the glass that was cloudy: it was more that the sphere was cloudy inside. He shook it gently. The cloudy contents swirled slowly like grey syrup. Will was baffled. The glass felt warm in his hand, comforting even. Despite its weird appearance, he instantly liked it. He slipped the sphere into his pocket and munched thoughtfully on a slice of green birthday cake.

As the others tidied up after tea, Will left the house quietly by the back door.

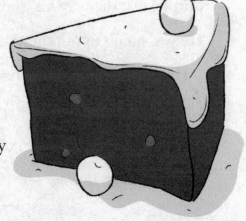

It was almost dark. He had made a decision. If Grandma could do what she liked on her birthday, so could he! Her words had come back to him: that elephant can be anything you want it to be. She didn't worry about rules and being zoological or anything else, so why should he? Will didn't care what Mrs Barnes or Isaac thought. He wanted his painting to be purple, just the way his grandma had liked it. He was going to put things right.

He turned out of the back gate down the alley. His heart was racing with excitement. He glanced up at Riya's house. He wondered about calling out to see if she'd keep him company, but the light in her bedroom window was off. For a second, he thought he saw the curtains twitch, but it was probably just a trick of the fading light.

Half an hour later, Will took a step back from the mural. He clamped the end of his paintbrush between his teeth and nodded. His painting was purple again. Wonderfully purple. Will added a final touch of yellow paint to the eternity symbol, blew out his cheeks and smiled.

'Well, Grandma, wherever you've gone, I hope you're proud of me,' he said to himself quietly.

All of a sudden, the outer edges of his painting began to glow. Will stumbled backwards in surprise. The eternity sign on the elephant's forehead burst into golden light. Will stared in fascination: all up and down the wall, the painted animals on the mural lit up and shone brightly. And then, to Will's astonishment, the elephant in front of him winked! Will shook his head in disbelief. Will shaded his eyes and squinted as he watched the glowing gates next to his elephant swing open slowly and gracefully.

Chapter
Three

Will stared through the open gates.
He realized immediately that there
was no hole in the wall; he wasn't looking into
the zoo. Instead, if he could believe his own
eyes, he was looking through a magical
entrance to somewhere else altogether. Will
stepped forwards carefully. The world beyond
the glowing gates seemed dark at first. Then

Will saw a few glowing dots of light bobbing in the darkness. He could make out giant shapes. What were they? He listened and could hear leaves rustling in the breeze. Will was fascinated. He didn't understand why, but he felt drawn to the strange world beyond the gates. He took a step closer and stopped.

'What are you doing?' he asked himself. He suddenly wanted to go home. His instincts told him to drop his brush and paint and run back as fast as possible. His route home flashed through his mind: a few dark streets, the alley, Riya's house, his back gate and home to safety, back where the world obeyed the rules.

Riya's house, thought Will and then a question popped into his head: what would Riya do? He didn't need to think for long. She wouldn't hesitate. She wouldn't run home. No chance. He remembered what she had said to him yesterday: where's your sense of adventure? She was right, he thought. She would go through this strange portal without a second thought. Grandma Rivers' words came back to him: all you need to do is believe.

Will gripped his paintbrush and stepped through the glowing gates into the night-time world beyond. He was plunged into a world of near darkness and stopped, waiting for his eyes to adjust. He realized that he was taking short, shallow breaths. The air felt a little cooler and fresher in his mouth and throat. The scents of fresh wood and damp earth filled his nostrils. He shifted his feet and realized that the ground beneath his feet was softer. The hard pavement, the heavy city air, the acrid exhaust fumes from moments earlier, all of it had disappeared. Even without being able to see properly, Will realized he was now somewhere quite different.

Suddenly, two dots of light bobbed and fluttered towards him. As they approached, Will could see that they looked and moved like butterflies. Except these butterflies were glowing and seemed to be made of nothing but pretty patterns of light. They fluttered close to Will's head. In alarm, he raised his arm to protect himself and hit himself on the head with his paintbrush.

'Ow!' he said. He rubbed his head and immediately felt a small bump. He looked at the paintbrush and almost dropped it in surprise. It had changed. It was thicker and heavier in his hand. It felt like plastic rather than wood and he could feel a switch under his thumb. He pressed down on the button. The object in his hand jolted powerfully and a brilliant beam of light suddenly illuminated his surroundings. Startled, Will released the button and the bright beam went out again. 'Whoa, that is one bright torch,' he said to himself. He pressed again, this time holding the button down firmly.

The torch throbbed with a mysterious energy
and the dazzling beam danced wildly over
his surroundings.

Will cast the
torch beam around in different
directions, although he wasn't sure whether he
was controlling it, or it was guiding his hand.

His finger and hand were also beginning
to ache.

He swivelled around on the
spot and tried to take in what he was seeing.

He was in a clearing surrounded by tall trees. At least they looked like trees. As he battled to keep the beam on one of them, Will noticed that the bark was frosty white, like an Arctic fox. To Will's astonishment, as he watched, the white bark peeled back from the trunk and branches to reveal what looked like words written in black on the wood underneath. Will tried to read the words, but his hand, wrist, and arm were throbbing with the effort of controlling the torch and he was forced to release the button.

At that moment, there was a noise behind him. Will spun round and found himself staring at four slender legs that stretched up higher than his head to a sandy-coloured body covered in brown patches.

Will stumbled backwards and fell onto his backside.

The giraffe in front of Will placed its two front legs far apart. It then lowered its long neck in one graceful movement until its chin was almost resting on the grass in front of Will. Will found himself staring into a pair of huge, masked eyes with long lashes.

'Why do giraffes have long necks?' said the giraffe.

Will nearly jumped out of his skin. 'You . . . you can talk,' he stammered.

The giraffe nodded slowly. 'Well?' it said. 'What d'you think? Why do we have long necks?'

Will glanced up at the giraffe's long curving neck. 'So you can reach leaves high up in the trees, right?' he answered.

The giraffe gave him a goofy grin. 'No, silly, it's because our feet smell!' Will blinked at him dumbly. The giraffe rolled its big, glistening eyes. 'Long neck, smelly feet. It's a joke, geddit?'

'Sure,' said Will uncertainly.

'I'm Sam,' said the giraffe. 'I'm a Spying Giraffe.'

'A Spying Giraffe?' repeated Will.

Sam continued, 'I'm really pleased to see you and be the first to say hello. Hello.'

'Hello,' said Will. 'My name's—'

Sam interrupted, 'The Night Zookeeper. Yes, we know. All the other giraffes are waiting to meet you. The Time-Travelling Elephant told us you were coming.'

'The time-travelling what?' said Will.

'You know—Maji!' said Sam.

Will shook his head again.

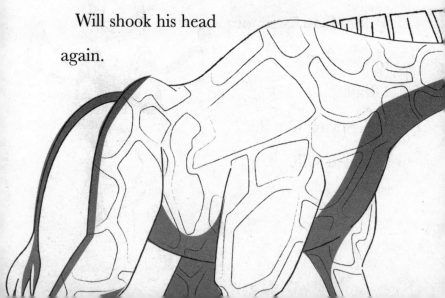

He wondered if he might be dreaming. After all, he was talking to a giraffe in a forest with trees like newspapers! He must be dreaming, he decided, until he felt a blast of humid breath ruffle his hair and a moist, muscular tongue lick him from his chin to his ear.

'Eeuw,' Will said, wiping gloopy dribble off his cheek. He clambered to his feet. 'What did you do that for?'

'Because you're the new Night Zookeeper!' replied the grinning giraffe.

'There must be a mistake,' said Will. 'I don't work at the zoo. I'm not a keeper. I've never even had a pet rabbit.'

Sam the Spying Giraffe cocked his head and examined Will. 'Well, why are you wearing that then?' he asked.

Will followed the giraffe's gaze to look down at his own clothes. 'Whoa!' he exclaimed. He was wearing a long blue coat over his school

56

clothes. There was an elephant symbol on the right sleeve of the coat. 'This isn't mine,' he muttered. He suddenly sensed something sitting on top of his head. He reached up and removed a peaked cap with the same symbol on the front panel. 'Nor is this,' he added.

'Told you so,' said Sam. 'Welcome to the Night Zoo. Thank you for coming to save us!'

Will frowned. 'Save you?' he said. 'Like I said, this must all

57

be a mistake.' He started to back away. 'Really, I'm not a Night Zookeeper. I'm no one special. I just go to school.' Walking backwards, Will stumbled over a root and his hand brushed against the trunk of a tree.

'Careful!' warned Sam.

'Can you show me the way back?' Will asked. He felt something cold and sticky on the back of his hand. He held his hand up and saw that it was covered in a thick, grey tar. A terrible smell wafted up from the sticky substance. 'Eeuw!' he said again. It smelt like a combination of drains, Grandma Rivers' favourite stinky cheese, and his little

58

brother's PE socks. Will looked at the tar-covered tree next to him. Broken branches lay scattered around the base of the trunk. Shrivelled leaves carpeted the ground. He glanced at other trees nearby. Many were ruined in the same way. Silky grey tar dripped from their bare branches and snaked down their trunks. He turned to Sam, who shook his head sadly.

'Now do you see why we need you, Night Zookeeper?' said the giraffe. And before Will could protect himself, Sam slurped his long tongue

up the side of Will's face again.

'Okay, enough with the licking,' said Will. 'I'm literally covered in dribble and tar!'

'Did you bring it with you?' asked Sam.

'Bring what?' replied Will.

'The Orb!' said the giraffe.

Will looked at him blankly and then his eyes flew open. Will rummaged in his shorts' pockets. Nothing. He stuck his hands into the deep pockets of his zookeeper's coat. His right hand closed around the sphere.

He pulled it out and held it up towards Sam. The giraffe's dark eyes sparkled with excitement. 'The Orb!' he cried in delight. 'Maji said she'd find a way of getting it to you. Come on. We can't waste time. Let's go!'

'Go? Go where?' asked Will, but the giraffe had already circled around and was galloping away towards the edge of the clearing.

Chapter
Four

'**S**am!' shouted Will. 'Wait a minute!
Where are you going?' But the giraffe
was already disappearing into the surrounding
trees. He couldn't believe how fast Sam could
run. Will suddenly felt slightly panicked. He
didn't want to be left alone in these strange
woods. The tar-stained trees gave him the
creeps. He stuck the Orb and the torch into

his coat pockets, broke
into a run, and dashed
after the galloping giraffe.

Will left the clearing and followed a narrow
track through the woods. It was darker under
the canopy of the trees. 'Sam, please. Slow
down!' Will called out. 'I can't keep up with
you.' Suddenly, a handful of glowing butterflies
swooped down from the branches above and
danced around Will's head. The path ahead
was lit up clearly. 'Thanks, guys,' said Will and
pushed on faster. 'Sam, where are you?' He
rounded a bend in the path and skidded
to a stop inches from Sam's tail.

'Shhh!' said Sam, without looking back at Will.

Will peered around the giraffe's flank to see why Sam might have stopped. 'What is it?' he said quietly.

'My ossicones are picking something up.'

'Your what?' asked Will.

Sam swung his head round to face Will. 'My ossicones. These little horn things on my head,' explained the giraffe. He looked serious. 'Yes, there's a definite tingling. It's my spy instincts kicking in.'

64

They waited in silence for a few seconds and then Will heard something. At first, he thought it was a breeze rippling through the leaves overhead, but then he was sure he could hear voices. It sounded like a hundred people all talking as quietly as possible under their breaths.

'Who is that?' asked Will nervously.

'The trees,' replied Sam. 'We're in the Whispering Wood. The trees are talking to each other, passing on news.'

Will strained to pick out any words from the babble of whispering voices. 'Can you tell what they're saying, Sam?' he asked.

'No, but my spy senses tell me it's not good. We need to keep going, but slowly and quietly, okay?'

Will nodded and they moved on deeper into the Whispering Wood.

Will's mind was a swirl of questions. As he walked alongside Sam, he spoke in hushed tones:

'Sam, where are we going?'

'To our camp. To all the other giraffes.'

'Are you all spies?'

'Yes, we are,' replied Sam proudly then hesitated. 'Although, technically, I'm not. Not yet.'

'Oh, how come?' asked Will.

'I'm still training,' said Sam with a sigh. 'Nneka—that's our leader—says I'm as clumsy as a bull in a china shop.'

'And what is this weird sphere-thingy?' asked Will. 'This gift from my grandma?'

Sam stopped for a few seconds and fixed his gaze on Will. 'It's called an Orb. It's a very special gift that only a Night Zookeeper has,' the giraffe replied.

'You've got to look after it, okay?' Sam looked really serious again.

Will nodded. 'What's it for?'

'To be honest, I'm not sure exactly,' said Sam. 'All I know is that it's really powerful and you put it against your forehead.'

Will looked down at the round object in his palm. He was about to lift it up to his head when he heard Sam say, 'Oh, look!'

Directly in front of them, a fallen tree trunk was blocking the path. It looked charred, as if it had been in a fire. But then Will noticed the slow-moving streams of sticky grey tar oozing from the bark. Will looked around. There

68

were many other fallen trees. The forest floor was a tangle of mangled branches and stained, crispy leaves. Nothing disturbed the silence that hung over them; the trees were no longer whispering. It was a scene of dark destruction.

Sam was shaking his head. His big eyes glistened in the torchlight. 'It's getting worse,' he said sadly. 'We must get home to the camp.' The giraffe tried to step over the fallen tree. Unfortunately, he got his long, slender legs in a tangle. For a moment, Will thought Sam was going to topple back on top of him; the giraffe swayed and tottered alarmingly before stumbling onto the far side.

'Phew!' said Sam. 'No harm done.' He lifted his neck and whacked his head on a branch overhead.

'Are you all right?' asked Will.

Sam nodded but looked embarrassed. 'Like a bull in a china shop, see?' he said.

'I think I'll go under,' said Will. Will dropped to his belly and crawled through a gap under the tree. He moved slowly, taking care not to get any of the tar on his zookeeper's cap and coat.

A short time later, Will and Sam arrived at a low wall made of loose rocks.

'We're here!' announced Sam.

Will peered over the wall and gasped. There

was a large clearing, full of
giraffes in a throng of spindly
legs, glossy hooves, and huge,
patchwork bodies. What was
even stranger was that all the giraffes
were standing completely still. Each
one had curled its neck round to rest
its head on its lower back.

'What's wrong with them?' he
asked anxiously.

'Shhh! Everyone's asleep,'
whispered Sam.

'You mean, you sleep standing
up?' said Will.

71

Sam nodded. 'Come on,' he said. 'Look, there's Nneka. She's on lookout.'

Sam stepped over the wall without getting too tangled up this time. 'Nneka!' he called out in a loud whisper. 'It's me, Sam!' Will clambered over too and saw a very tall giraffe padding forwards to meet Sam.

'I am pleased to see you are safe, Sam,' said Nneka. 'What news do you have?'

Sam was beaming from ear to ear. 'Guess who I found,' he said.

'Sam, please, this is no time for games,' replied Nneka sternly. 'Or one of your jokes, or—'

Nneka cut herself off as Will stepped out

from behind Sam. He held up his hand and gave a short wave. 'Hi,' he said. Nneka's huge, liquid eyes opened wide.

'Night Zookeeper!' she said. 'You found the new Night Zookeeper!' Sam raised his chin. He looked as proud

as a peacock. 'Welcome, you are so welcome!' exclaimed Nneka, smiling at Will. 'And just in time too. Now you can help us fight back at last!'

Will felt a little awkward: Nneka seemed so pleased to see him. More and more questions bubbled round his head. One ballooned larger than the others: who or what was he supposed to fight? He glanced at the back of his hand. It was still smeared with the sticky tar. 'Is this all to do with this horrible stuff?' he asked. 'It's all over the woods.'

Nneka frowned. 'Void Gunk,' she sighed. 'Is this true, Sam? Have you seen more of it?'

Sam nodded. 'It's much worse than before, Nneka. They must be close,' he confirmed.

Will felt a trickle of fear snake down his back. 'Please, I don't understand,' he said. 'Who must be close? What's a Void?'

'They're robots. They look like giant spiders,' explained Nneka. 'They try to kidnap the Night Zoo animals, and the gunk they leave behind destroys the woods.' Will could hear the fear and disgust in her voice. 'Most of the animals are in hiding. There are usually clouds of Bumbling Bees in the forest at this time of year. Now there are none. Along with the Green Squirrels, the Racer Robins, everyone's gone.'

Sam suddenly raised his head and his whole body went rigid. 'Oh dear,' he said. 'My ossicones, Nneka. They're going crazy!'

Nneka lifted her head and sensed the air too. 'You're right, Sam. There is something!' she said in a low voice. 'How stupid of me! I wasn't concentrating.'

'What is it?' Will asked in a whisper.

There was a rustling noise just the other

side of the wall. Will's heart leapt in his chest. He peeked over the top of the wall into the darkness. A few Night Butterflies were resting on the trunk of a nearby tree. Will could make out the peeling white bark. It was one of those weird newspaper trees again. In the dull light

from the butterflies, Will could just about read the words as the papery bark peeled away: DANGER NEAR.

Suddenly, a loud clank broke the quiet of the Whispering Wood. It was the sound of moving metal.

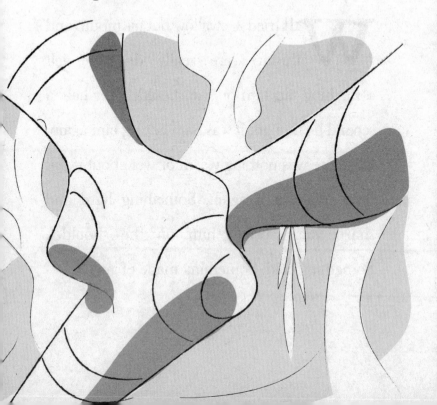

Chapter Five

Will tried to swallow but his mouth and throat were really dry. He felt something tap him on the shoulder. For half a second he thought it was Sam licking him again, but there was nothing warm or wet about it this time. Will felt it again. Something hard and sharp was tapping him on the shoulder. Something cold. Something made of metal.

Sam's voice boomed in his ear, 'Void! It's a Void!'

Will spun round and his heart leapt into his mouth. He stood face to face with a giant, metallic spider. An angry red light glowed in the centre of its gunmetal head. Glistening tar was dripping in pulses from its sharp fangs.

Its black body was made of cold steel. Will was almost frozen with fear: the Void was even worse than he had imagined.

There was an explosion of noise as the giraffes woke up and rushed around in confusion and alarm. Nneka called out to them, 'Everyone stay together! Stay close!' The giraffes quickly gathered around Will, Sam, and Nneka, all staring in fear at the Void.

Clicker-clacker! Clicker-clacker!

The Void clicked and clacked its fangs together and crouched low to the ground. It looked ready to pounce. At that very moment, there was a terrible hissing sound behind them. Will realized with horror that the first Void had distracted them on purpose: four more Voids with burning red eyes had sneaked into the camp from the far side. Immediately, the giraffes began to panic.

One of the Voids leapt into the air towards the group. As it passed high over all of their heads, the Void spun a cable behind it. Another Void leapt over them, leaving behind another curving cable. And then the Voids seemed to come from all sides, spinning their cables furiously.

Clicker-clacker!

The first Void, the leader, urged them on. Too late Will realized what the Voids were doing: they were all going to be trapped inside a web of metal.

The giraffes were now charging about in panic. Will was suddenly knocked sideways by a flying hoof and he stumbled into the wall. As he steadied himself, his hand closed around one of the smaller rocks. Without thinking, Will picked the rock up and threw it as hard as he could at the Void Leader. The rock arced across the clearing and struck the Void flush on the side of its head. The giant spider machine snapped its head round to stare directly at Will.

Its red eye narrowed and it scuttled forwards towards him, its front legs raised menacingly.

Will tried to move, but his legs refused. For several seconds, he watched helplessly as the Void Leader closed the distance between them. Suddenly, he felt himself lifted off his feet and thrown sideways. Sam had grabbed the collar of Will's jacket with his teeth and had tossed Will over the wall, clear of the danger and the Voids' web. Miraculously, Will landed on his feet. 'Run!' shouted Sam, who was clambering clumsily over the wall. Will broke into a sprint between the trees. 'Keep running!' urged Sam, galloping up beside him. Somewhere close behind them, there was a loud hiss. 'Don't look back! Just keep going!'

Will did as he was told. His heart was pounding, his breathing ragged but fear was firing the muscles in his legs, driving him on.

He plunged through a narrow gap between two tree trunks, but tripped on a root. He sprawled to the ground, landing with a hard blow that knocked the air out of his chest. In the gloom, Will looked up from the earth for Sam. The galloping giraffe hadn't noticed Will fall over; he was charging away through the woods.

'Sam!' wheezed Will. 'Stop!'

Within just a few seconds, the air began to glow with red light. Still fighting for breath, Will sat up and twisted round searching for the danger. He tried to stand up, but his burnt-out legs protested and he crumpled to the earth again. And then he spotted it: a slit of harsh, crimson light focused directly on him was approaching rapidly between the trees.

Clicker-clacker, Clicker-clacker.

The Void Leader gnashed its fangs together and leapt into the air. Will ducked and the metal creature passed over his head. A glistening cable formed inches above him. Before Will could react, the Void jumped again and again, back and forth. It worked at incredible speed, weaving the cables into a prison.

'No, no, no!' said Will. He tried to think of something he could do, but his mind was a mess. He thrust his hands into his pockets, frantically searching for anything to defend himself with. His fingers closed around the torch and he whipped it out and pressed the button. The torch bucked violently in his hand as the bright beam burst out. The Void Leader hissed loudly. Will tried to focus the beam on the metal creature above him. The light swept across the trees overhead, illuminating the canopy. Out of the corner of his eye, Will noticed a number of huge drooping flowers the size of a church bells amongst the leafy branches. And then, just as Will managed to light up the Void, to his horror, the shuddering torch slipped from his sweaty grip. The torch went out, fell to the ground and started to roll. Will lurched forwards to grab it but the torch picked up speed and rolled between a gap in the criss-crossed cage. Will stuck his arm through the gap, straining his shoulder against the hot metal cables, reaching, reaching for the torch which now lay just a fingertip out of reach.

'Help!' Will shouted. 'Someone help!' Tears pricked his eyes. 'Sam! Anyone!' Although his vision was blurry, Will thought he saw a dark shape moving rapidly through the trees. He wiped his eyes and blinked. Someone else was in the Whispering Wood! Someone dashing and weaving towards him. Someone with silvery-purple hair! 'Riya?' he said in astonishment.

'Will!' came the reply.

Chapter Six

From between the bars of the spider's cage, Will saw his friend appear through the trees. He had never been so pleased to see anyone in his life.

'Riya, help!' he said. 'I'm trapped!' Riya skidded to a halt. Her mouth dropped open as she saw the giant metal monster. 'Get me out of here, please,' urged Will.

Riya's eyes darted around the scene, taking in the details. She called out, 'And what exactly can I do about this situation?' The Void Leader glared at Riya and hissed. It raised its fangs and squirted two streams of glossy grey tar in her direction. Riya leapt out of the way nimbly. 'I can't get any closer!' she said.

Will felt dizzy with fear and frustration. He held the bars of his cage and rested his forehead against the cooling metal, trying to think. A memory stirred in his mind. His forehead. Something about his forehead! Will thrust his hands into his coat pocket. His fingers touched something round. Suddenly,

Sam's words came back to him: the Orb was powerful and special! But, what had Sam told him to do with it? Put it against your forehead, he thought, that was it! Will took the Orb in both hands and lifted it to his forehead. He pressed it gently against his skin.

Immediately, there was a change inside the Orb. The cloudy greyness inside burst into a rainbow of colours. Will suddenly felt strangely calm. The jumble of worries in his head melted away. He looked up. The Void was still at work. It was scuttling over his cage, strengthening the dome with more and more cables. But somehow Will wasn't panicked by this any more. It was almost as if it were happening to someone else. Fragments of a picture, like pieces of a jigsaw, began to float around his mind. To his astonishment, the fragments began to join together and take shape inside the Orb. A shape emerged within the swirling colours. To Will's surprise, it was a small plastic pot with a strange plant in it. He recognized it immediately. The image inside the sphere was his own Venus flytrap! The picture of the plant dissolved and Will lowered the Orb. He felt a surge of confidence. The Orb had given him an idea.

Will called out to his friend, 'Riya, can you see those big flowers up there?'

Riya looked up into the branches and grimaced. 'Uh-huh. Wow, they look nasty,' she said. 'Like one of your weird plants.'

Will nodded vigorously. 'Yes, like my Venus flytrap.'

'Or spidertrap!' Riya exclaimed. 'Don't worry, I get what you're thinking.' She clenched her jaw and leapt into a nearby newspaper tree. The white bark immediately curled aside to reveal the words:

OI!
GET OFF!

Will watched with nervous admiration as Riya climbed gracefully higher into the tree. When she reached a thick branch near the top of the tree, she stood upright and stepped out along it. The branch bent under her weight, but she kept her nerve. She placed one foot in front of the other, like a cat on a garden fence. Will found himself holding his breath.

High above him, Riya had reached one of the enormous, drooping flowers. It had hinged jaws lined with long spikes. The flower hung from a single, towering stem. Riya took a deep breath and leapt from the end of the branch across the thin air to the flower. She wrapped her arms and clamped her legs around the top of it. Immediately, the thick stem began to bend under the extra weight. Riya and the flower plunged down towards the Void Leader on top of Will's cage. The Void looked up just in time to see the giant flower swooping down towards it. Its red eye flashed in alarm and it tried to scuttle away. The spikes on the flower brushed the Void's metal back. The flower snapped shut just around the Void's body. The Void hissed and gnashed its fangs. The bent stem creaked like the string of a bow, desperate to spring back into its natural shape.

Riya grinned down at Will. 'Give me a countdown then,' she said. 'Three!'

'Two! One!' shouted Will enthusiastically.

Riya released her grip and leapt aside onto the ground. Like a catapult, the huge flower stem pinged back up with incredible speed. The trapped Void was whipped into the air. At the top of the swing, the flower's jaws opened and the Void was thrown free. It hissed and squealed as it was launched up through the

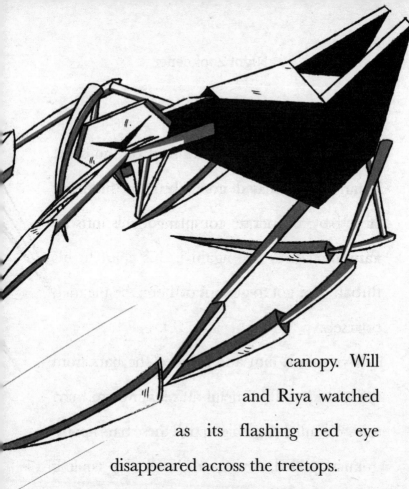

canopy. Will and Riya watched as its flashing red eye disappeared across the treetops.

Riya rushed over to Will.

'That was amazing!' he exclaimed.

Riya shrugged her shoulders casually.

'Your idea,' she replied.

Will grabbed two of the bars of the cage. Now the Void had gone, he was suddenly struck by the close confines of his prison. Panic began to rise again in his chest to his throat. 'I've got to get out of here,' he pleaded hoarsely.

Riya joined him and gripped the bars from the outside. 'The metal. It's still warm,' she said. 'We might be able to pull these bars apart.'

They pulled, trying to bend the cooling metal. However, they only managed to prise the bars apart a few inches before Will felt the strength going from his arms.

'It's no good,' he said forlornly.

'We've got to work together,' urged Riya. 'Don't give up. Pull at the same time.'

Will gritted his teeth and he and Riya strained at the bars until their arms and shoulders ached. Slowly but surely they made a narrow hole between the two bars. Will sized it up. He felt a rush of excitement. It would be a tight fit, but . . .

'I think I can get out,' he said breathlessly. He passed his cap through the hole to Riya and stuck his head through. Next, he squeezed his shoulders through the gap and then began to worm the rest of his body through. Riya grabbed the collar of his coat and pulled.

'You can do, it, Will,' she encouraged him.

For a horrible moment, Will thought he was stuck as his hips caught on the bars. He wriggled and twisted and suddenly he was free! He tumbled out of the cage and flopped onto the ground. He heaved a sigh of relief. 'Thank you,' he said, grinning up at Riya.

At that moment, Sam burst through the trees. 'Night Zookeeper! Where are you?' said the giraffe. He spotted Will and then Riya. 'Oh, who are you? Did I miss something?'

Will stared up at Sam from the ground. 'Kinda. Sam, this is my friend, Riya.'

Sam noticed the metal cage. 'The Void!

What happened?'

'It's all right. Riya catapulted it across the forest. You should have seen it!'

'Thank you, Riya! You saved the Night Zookeeper!' said Sam. His long, blue tongue flopped out of his mouth.

'Whoa, what are you doing?' asked Riya. She realized too late. Sam slurped his tongue up her face.

Dribble glistened in her hair.

Riya screwed up her face. 'Are you serious?' she exclaimed, and Will chuckled.

Sam grinned. 'The Void. Which way did it go?' he asked.

Will got to his feet gingerly. 'I'm not sure. That way I think,' he said.

Sam's eyes widened. 'You mean back towards the camp?'

'Oh,' said Will. 'We didn't exactly have time to aim.'

'We've got to go!' urged Sam. 'You need to save the others.'

'Hang on a sec,' said Will and

looked around quickly. 'There you are,' he added and picked up the torch.

Will, Riya, and Sam set off back towards the giraffe camp as quickly and quietly as possible. Several Night Butterflies circled them, lighting the way.

'I thought I was imagining it when I saw you,' Will told Riya. 'How did you get here?'

'I saw you in the alley behind my house. I followed you through those glowing gates,' explained Riya.

Will filled Riya in on everything that had happened so far.

'By the way, it worked, Sam,' said Will. 'The Orb. I didn't know what to do, but then I saw my Venus flytrap inside it. It made me think about trapping the Void.'

'I told you it was special,' said Sam. 'Look, I think we're nearly there. There's the wall. Shoo!' Sam blew a couple of times at the butterflies and they disappeared into the treetops.

Will and Riya crouched low to the ground as they approached the rocky wall. Behind them, Sam lowered his neck and head to their level and tried to tiptoe on his hooves. He lost his balance for a moment and banged his snout into Riya's shoulder. She gave him an exasperated look.

'Aren't you a bit, you know, tall to be a spy?' she hissed. 'And clumsy!'

Will was peeking over the top of the rocks. 'That's not good,' he muttered. Riya and Sam joined him. In the clearing, all the other giraffes were trapped under a giant metal cage. The Voids were patrolling the perimeter. Will heard Nneka's voice: 'Let us go! We will not give in to Nulth!'

The Voids all stopped moving and began to gnash their fangs in a frenzy:

Clicker-clacker!   Clicker-clacker!

Will spotted the Void Leader they had defeated before. It had found its way back to the camp. Will was pleased to see that there was a dent in its metal and one of its fangs had been snapped off.

It clambered up the outside of the cage and hissed and swiped at Nneka. Sticky tar spurted from its fang onto the giraffes below, who jostled and pushed against each other in panic.

'We have to rescue them,' said Will.

'Yes, but how? We're outnumbered,' said Riya. 'And that cage will be cold soon.'

'I don't know, but we've got to try,' he insisted.

'Ooh, I've just had an idea,' said Sam.

'Great!' said Will.

Will and Riya both looked at the giraffe expectantly for several seconds.

'Well?' they both said.

'Oh, sorry, yes. I don't think I've mentioned this before. Or perhaps I have, I can't remember,' said Sam.

'What? Mentioned what?'

'Did I mention I can turn myself invisible?'

Will and Riya exchanged a look of surprise.

'No, Sam, you didn't,' said Will.

'Are you sure?' asked Sam. 'I must have told

you. I am a spy after all!'

'I think I would have remembered!' replied

Will.

'Whatever, guys,' interrupted

Riya. 'What's the plan

then, Sam?'

Chapter Seven

Sam closed his big, dark eyes. Nothing happened. He squeezed his eyelids together. 'There!' he announced.

'Um, Sam, we can still see you,' said Riya.

Sam opened one eye and peeked down at himself. 'Yes, so you can,' he said.

'Sam, are you sure you can do this?' asked Will.

'Shhh, I just need to concentrate,' he replied and shut his eyes firmly again. And again nothing happened. Riya rolled her eyes and was about to say something when Sam started to change. The outline of the giraffe's body from his hooves to his tail to the tips of his ossicones began to glow. It reminded Will of his glowing elephant painting. At the same time, Sam's body became more and more transparent until Will and Riya could see right through him. Then, after a final flash, the giraffe's glowing outline faded. Sam had disappeared.

'Sam?' whispered Will.

He felt a snort of warm breath on his cheek. Will smiled. 'Don't even think about licking me!' he said firmly.

Riya reached out a hand into the thin air. She almost jumped as her fingers made contact with something solid but unseen. She patted Sam's invisible leg. 'Wow, that's really cool, Sam,' said Riya. 'And that doesn't mean you can lick me either!'

'Are you ready?' came Sam's voice. Will and Riya nodded. 'I'll distract the Voids for as long as possible,' he said.

'Are you sure about this?' Riya whispered to Will. 'It's just, Sam . . . well, there's a reason he's still a trainee, right?'

'Hey, I heard that,' said Sam. He sounded hurt.

'Don't worry, Sam, you can do it,' Will reassured him. 'Just remember, less bull in a china shop, more graceful as a swan, okay?'

Invisible Sam crept forward into the camp and slowly stood up on his back legs. He picked up six rocks from the wall with his front hooves. He wobbled and nearly dropped them. Sam turned to face the giant cage and the Voids. He took a deep breath, got himself nicely balanced and then he started to juggle.

He launched the first rock into the air.
And then the next and the next and
the next until he was juggling all six
rocks in a circle, faster and faster. The
effect was magical. Hypnotic. The
rocks seemed to be flying round and
round in the air by themselves.

All the Voids had turned to watch. They seemed to be in a trance. They stood in a line watching the circling rocks. Their red eyes were dull and their fangs hung limply from their jaws. As Sam continued to juggle the rocks, the Voids began to rotate their heads round and round following the circling rocks.

'It's working!' whispered Will.

Sam was having difficulty balancing. He tottered about on his back legs. However, with great effort, he started to back away towards the other side of the clearing, away from the giant cage. The mesmerised Voids plodded after the magical, spinning rocks.

'Look, Sam's leading them away,' said Riya.

'Now's our chance,' said Will. Next to him lay a long, thick branch that a Void had smashed off a tree. He picked up one end and Riya grabbed the other. They crept over the rocky wall and dashed towards the giraffes, carrying the branch between them. They stopped by the cage out of view of Sam and the Voids.

'Nneka!' whispered Will as loudly as he dared. Some of the giraffes looked round in surprise and began to grunt and snort.

'Quiet everyone,' commanded Nneka. She swung her head down towards the two children.

'Night Zookeeper, you have returned. We knew you would.'

'Don't worry, we'll get you out of here,' said Will.

Riya was feeling the metal bars of the giant cage. 'It's getting cold, Will,' she said. Will thrust one end of the branch between two vertical bars. Then, as planned, they both grabbed the loose end and pulled, levering the strong branch against the metal. Slowly, they began to prise the bars apart. The giraffes whispered with excitement. Will and Riya pulled and pulled against the lever and the gap widened further.

Suddenly one of the giraffes cried with alarm, 'Look! Poor Sam!'

Will let go of the branch and rushed around the side of the cage. His heart leapt in his chest: Sam was still juggling the rocks but he wasn't completely invisible any more! Worse still, Sam hadn't noticed. He had led the Voids to the far side of the camp. Without realizing, Sam had backed into a tree covered in Void Gunk. Grey tar was smeared across his coat and up his neck. The Voids were fanning out to surround him;

it was clear that they could see him again. The awful gnashing of metal fangs filled the night air.

Clicker-clacker!

The sound broke Sam's concentration. The rocks fell out of their orbit and tumbled to the ground.

There was a flash and Sam was whole again for everyone to see. The Void Leader's eye glowed with excitement and it immediately launched a jet of sticky tar into Sam's face. The other Voids joined in, squirting ribbons of the disgusting gunk all over Sam's neck and body.

The poor young giraffe looked terrified. Void Gunk dripped from his chin and dribbled down his neck and his long legs started to see-saw beneath him. Worse still, Sam seemed to be fading. Not like before. He wasn't becoming invisible. The colours were draining from Sam's coat, which became a patchwork of different shades of grey. Suddenly Sam was looking directly at Will through the crowd of Voids. Will saw the look of fear and helplessness on Sam's face. And then, to his dismay, Will saw the light in Sam's eyes fading as they became dull and unfocused. The young giraffe tottered drunkenly for a second or two before he keeled over in a heap on the ground.

'NO!' shouted Will at the top of his voice. He glanced back quickly at Riya, who was still trying to prise open the giraffes' cage. Will was on his own. No one else was going to save Sam. No one else could help his friend. Will could hear his own pulse throbbing in his ears. Sam's words came back to him: you're the new Night Zookeeper. Thank you for coming to save us. Will gritted his teeth. Sam was right. It was down to him. This was his purpose here in this strange world of the Night Zoo. He reached into the deep pockets of his coat. His fingers closed around a piece of card. It was the gift tag from Grandma Rivers' present. The words on it made sense now: From Here Begins the Battle. And then Will found his torch. Ignoring his doubts and his fears and his thumping heart, Will sprinted across the clearing and shouted at the top of his voice: 'Oi! Leave my friend alone!'

Chapter
Eight

Will held the torch out in front of him like a sword. He held down the button and the brilliant beam cut through the night air. Will aimed the beam directly at Sam and the Voids. Every one of the Voids paused and scuttled round to face him. Their red eyes narrowed as if they were squinting. Will gripped the torch as firmly as he could and kept his aching thumb pressed down hard on the button. To his surprise, the white light from the torch began to change. Jagged shafts of light—like orange, blue, green, and purple lightning—fizzed along the main beam. The Voids hissed angrily. One began to back away.

In the middle, Sam was bathed in the kaleidoscope of colours. His collapsed body began to stir. He lifted his head and colour flooded back to his coat. His huge, dark eyes shone brightly. The Voids stumbled back in shock as Sam rose majestically to his full height. His whole body was now surrounded by a halo of honey-coloured light.

Despite the effort, Will kept the torch focused on Sam. He saw Sam wink at him as the giraffe's body became as bright as a beacon in the woods. 'It's just like the purple elephant,' he said to himself in amazement. The Whispering Wood was suddenly a riot of colour and noise. The newspaper trees around the camp glowed and the headlines on their trunks announced: the Night Zookeeper has arrived! Fluorescent flowers burst from the forest floor adding to the colourful spectacle. Suddenly, Will became aware of someone next to him. He glanced to his side and saw Riya standing by him. She put a hand on his shoulder.

'What's happening?' she asked in awe.

'I don't know,' he replied. 'Everything seems so alive!'

There was a dazzling light behind them. They swung round towards the giant metal cage.

All of the huddled giraffes were glowing, surrounded by the same golden light as Sam. There was a groan of metal. The prison around the giraffes began to creak and bend. The giraffes shone brighter and brighter until suddenly a bar pinged away from the cage. Within seconds, the rest of the cage snapped apart and tumbled to the ground.

Immediately, the giraffes galloped forward and stood proudly in a line behind Will and Riya. From every direction, other animals charged into the camp. Bumbling Bees, Green Squirrels, Racer Robins, even a line of Howler Ants: all the forest creatures that had been

hiding from the Voids rushed to join Will, Riya, and the giraffes. They buzzed and yelped, snapped and howled, and lined up to face the enemy. A cloud of pure white light as bright as the moon formed above the giraffes as a thousand Night Butterflies took to the air, their delicate wings and bodies gleaming. The light that filled the camp was now almost blinding!

Will smiled. He didn't feel alone or scared any more. Instead, he concentrated the torch beam on the enemy. The damaged Void Leader rose onto its back legs and pointed at Will. It was the order to attack.

The Voids started to cross the camp, but they seemed uncertain and moved slowly.

'Charge!' ordered Will in reply and ran straight towards the Voids. Will aimed the torch beam at the Void Leader. The powerful light burst off its dented metal, which began to glow and warp. The Void Leader skittered around in a circle, trying to turn away from the beam. It squealed as smoke billowed from its joints. Suddenly, it could take no more and it scurried away over the wall and into the woods. With their leader vanquished, the other Voids were suddenly all fleeing, desperate to escape the intense, colourful light. They too turned and disappeared at speed into the woods.

For a few seconds, the camp was completely quiet, before a huge cheer broke out. Will and Riya ran towards Sam, and Will threw his arms around the giraffe's neck.

'You saved me,' said Sam.

'I was so scared when you fell down,' admitted Will quietly, hugging Sam's neck a little more firmly.

'It was horrible, Night Zookeeper,' said Sam. 'I never want to feel like that again. It felt like all the colour and joy and silliness and freedom and imagination were being sucked out of the world. Everything was grey. I even felt grey!'

'I'm so happy you're all right,' said Will. 'And, Sam, you don't have to call me Night Zookeeper. Call me Will.'

'But we're not really allowed,' said Sam with a frown. 'It's against the rules.'

Will was surprised by the words he heard himself saying in reply: 'I don't care. I reckon not following rules is good sometimes! Everyone told me my painting should be grey. But I made it purple and I was right. None of this would have happened if I'd done a boring, obvious elephant, would it? So, you can one hundred percent break the rules and call me Will, okay?'

Sam beamed with pride.

'Are you sure you're all right, Sam?' asked Riya with concern. She was examining the small remaining patches of Void Gunk on the giraffe's coat, neck, and face.

'Oh, it's nothing a good lick won't cure,' Sam replied with his goofy grin. 'Watch!' Sam stuck his huge blue tongue out and swung it all the way up to his ear.

He stuck the tip inside his ear and rummaged around, cleaning away the gunk.

'Wow, Sam, that is so gross!' said Riya, and Will laughed out loud.

Nneka trotted up next to them. 'You did it, Night Zookeeper!' she said.

Will puffed his cheeks and blew out. 'Whoa, that was intense, but it wasn't just me,' Will replied. 'All of us. We did it together.'

Another giraffe called out from the edge of the camp, 'Nneka! Night Zookeeper! Come and see this.'

Will, Riya, and Sam jogged over to the camp wall. There was a group of newspaper trees close by. The white bark on their trunks was curling back to reveal a new headline. Will could see the same words in bold letters on each of them:

FEAR
IN FIRE
DESERT!

'The Fire Desert!' said Sam. 'But that's so far away!'

'This is not good news,' said Nneka, shaking her head. 'I never thought this evil would reach other parts of the Night Zoo.'

'You mean there are Voids in the desert too?' said Will.

'It's almost certain,' Nneka replied.

'Well, now we know where to go next,' said Sam brightly.

'No, Sam,' said Nneka. 'This is something Will must do. It's the Night Zookeeper's duty.'

Sam looked crestfallen. 'Please, Nneka,' pleaded Sam. 'I want to go. I don't want Will and Riya to have all the fun saving the Night Zoo. Please!'

'You've got a funny idea of fun, Sam,' said Riya.

'Nneka, I'd really like Sam to come with us too,' said Will. 'We need his help.'

Nneka sighed. 'Very well, Night Zookeeper.'

'So how do we get to this desert then?' asked Will.

'It's right on the other side of the Night Zoo,' explained Sam. 'I could carry you there but it would take days!'

'So, what do we do?' asked Will. 'Any ideas? Anyone?' The giraffes frowned and shrugged.

Riya was deep in thought. Suddenly, her dark eyes flashed. 'I've got an idea,' she said with a smile. 'Remember when we didn't know what to do last time? When you were stuck in the cage?'

'Of course, the Orb!' Will cried and stuck his hand into his pocket. He pressed the Orb to his forehead. It filled with coloured lights.

Shapes started to emerge. 'That's it, that's it!' he whispered. The image became clearer, but this time it wasn't a single object. Instead, two images shimmered inside the swirling cloud of colours: the first was his torch and the second was a golden eternity sign. Will lowered the Orb. His eyes flew open.

'I think I know what to do,' he said excitedly. 'I painted that symbol with my paintbrush. And when I came through the gates, my paintbrush turned into this!' He held up his torch. He paused for a second and then flicked the switch. The torch jolted in his hand as the powerful beam shot out.

Will struggled to hold on to it as the beam moved across the night sky. The torch seemed to be guiding his hand and the beam was carving out a blazing symbol in the darkness above: a huge eternity symbol. Will, Riya, and the giraffes watched in awe as a strange landscape started to appear within the floating symbol: a huge expanse of moonlit sand; a long snaking dune; and a silvery lake surrounded by palms. Most strangely, spiralling columns of flames like whirling, fiery trees dotted the desert landscape.

They all stared at the Fire Desert beyond the portal.

Will turned to his friends. 'Well, what are we waiting for?' he asked.

'I'm not so sure, Will,' said Riya with a frown. 'Those fires look seriously dangerous.'

'Where's your sense of adventure gone now?' he asked her with a grin.

She wrinkled her nose. 'Very clever,' she said. 'Good point.'

As the giraffes called out messages of good luck, Will the new Night Zookeeper, Riya, and Sam stepped side by side through the portal and into their next adventure.

Joshua Davidson

By night, Joshua Davidson is the head Night Zookeeper. He works in the Night Zoo and cares for many magical animals such as Purple Octocows and Banana Hedgehogs. During his nightly rounds he enjoys playing memory games with the Time-Travelling Elephant and hide-and-seek with the Spying Giraffes. Sadly he is yet to win a single game in either contest.

By day, he is an author, artist, game designer, and tech entrepreneur. He came up with the idea for nightzookeeper.com, a website where anyone can draw animals and write stories about them, whilst studying an MA in Digital Art at Norwich University of the Arts.

Josh introduced the Night Zoo to Paul, Buzz, Phil, and Sam and together they built the Night Zookeeper website. It has since been nominated for a BAFTA, won a London Book Fair award, and is currently used in thousands of schools across the world to inspire amazing creative writing.

Buzz Burman

Buzz studied graphic design in Norwich, England where he met Night Zookeeper Josh. Many years later, Josh brought Buzz to the gates of the Night Zoo. Ever since then he has been the regular painter and decorator in the zoo. He draws on his gigantic imagination to care for the animals there and to explore new parts of the world!

By day, Buzz is a designer and illustrator with a love of clever ideas. As well as drawing what the animals look like in this book, he also designed the cover, the Night Zookeeper website, and Night Zookeeper logo!

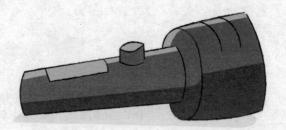

Create your own magical animals

At nightzookeeper.com you can test your powers of creativity and invent your own magical zoo animals. Just like CreativePug5 and Maiab have done in these Zoo reports.

Zoo report:

The Shadows of the Night Zoo
by CreativePug5

Hello everyone, NZK CreativePug5 here, with a Night Zoo update for you:

The Shadows of the Night Zoo is an animal that follows you around all the time, and you don't know it! He has no name so we just call him The Shadow Master. The Shadow Master used to be a beautiful bird in the Night Zoo but one day he broke free of the Zoo and we could never find him. He has been spotted recently however, three times, flying over Clock Woods in the north.

Once myself and the other Night Zookeepers saw a glimpse of a massive shadow over a pile of orbs in a little nest! Then we found out something quite miraculous about The Shadow Master, that he didn't lay eggs but ORBS!!!!!!!!!!!

It is unclear why he left the Zoo. The zookeepers

had done everything to try and make him happy. He was our best bird in the Night Zoo. Now he has vanished into the shadows: just a shadow following YOU all the time. So you'd better watch out!

Zoo report:

Samuel the Speedy, Sprightly Snail
by Maiab

Sam—also known as Samuel the Speedy, Sprightly Snail—is a lively, dynamic, old chap who is much quicker than any other snail that ever lived. He is a deep azure colour, signaling that he would be a highly poisonous bit of escargot. His shell, you ask? Oh yes, it is the unbreakable, limited-edition, coffee-brown Sublime Shelly 2000 he received as a birthday gift from his old friend Barney the Blissful, Blithesome Beetle. This bubbly snail lives on more flat terrain than his other relatives, who have decided to dwell in the plants and in trees. You'd assume this fellow would stop wiggling about at his age, but no, for he is a very speedy, sprightly snail indeed, like his name suggests. Just keep in mind that at times he will ignore you because he is, for a strange reason, enjoying every second of his life, even when people have to strap him down to the floor because he's so energetic.

How to create a magical animal

Use the questions below as a guide in creating your own magical animal. We've added in our own examples to show you how it's done.

What is your animal's name?
Sam the Spying Giraffe

What does your animal like to eat?
Vegetable soup (this helps Sam to turn invisible).

Where does your animal live?
Sam lives in the Whispering Woods in the Night Zoo.

Does your animal have any friends?
Yes! His best friends are Will and Riya.
They love going on adventures together!

What does your animal dislike?

Sam dislikes evil Voids that try to sneak into the Night Zoo and scare his fellow magical animals.

Does your animal have a special ability?

Yes! He can turn invisible, which makes him incredibly good when playing hide and seek!

Now it's your turn!

Visit **nightzookeeper.com** to create your own magical animal on a computer or tablet. Or simply create it on paper.

Discover a new part of the Night Zoo

In this story, Aubrey124 has imagined a secret part of the Night Zoo, somewhere closed to visitors, where a whole host of unique creatures live . . .

The New Night Zoo
by Aubrey124

Through the Night Zoo there is a small forest of flowers and trees built together to make a small path to the other end of the Zoo that is not open to visitors or any unauthorized animals. It is full of Teleportation Bats, deep caves, angry Speed Bears, Glowing Fish, and endless pits of darkness.

The Teleportation Bats can teleport to anywhere in the exhibit within the blink of an eye. There is a big enclosure for the Speed Bears. They constantly try to break the enclosure open by ramming into it. They feed off of the Glowing Fish, as this gives them the power to run at extraordinary speeds.

No one has seen this area of the Night Zoo before, the path is a secret as you can barely see it. The caves are long and quiet. Everything echoes down long dreary paths of the cave. You can get lost quite easily because it is dark. You can leave a trail of breadcrumbs but the animals will pick it up just as you put it down.

In the caves, water drips down from the ceiling and taps your head like a woodpecker.

The Teleportation Bats screech at you as you pass. They are territorial and mean. If you attempt to catch one they will quickly teleport away. The Speed Bears ignore the bats and hate their own enclosure. The enclosure stands next to a water pit. The caves are across the land where the bats nest and rest to go out at night. The caves glow during the day because you can see the bright red eyes of the bats staring down the cave.

There is a space for the Speed Bears to get out of their enclosure by the exit path. It is a lit-up area and large enough to fit the gigantic beasts. Through the path, there is a great land awaiting the visitor as they arrive. The Glowing Fish live in a bright, blinding river. They multiply by the day and are prey to the Speed Bears.

They have circular fins and a triangle -shaped head. This part of the Night Zoo is a secret and is yet to be discovered.

Invent a new magical location!

Once you have created a magical animal, they will need a place to live. Can you invent a new location in the Night Zoo? Use these words to help you.

Locations

Volcano

Desert

Beach

Mountain

Waterfall

Ocean

City

Village

River

Jungle

Temple

Tower

Adjectives

Giant

Bright

Mystical

Dazzling

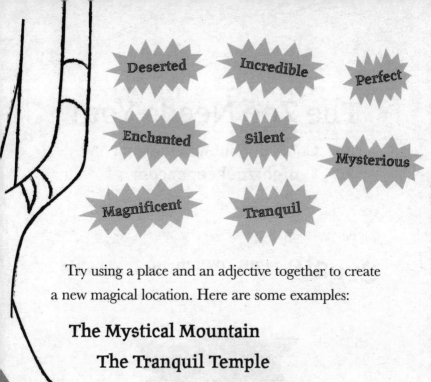

Deserted

Incredible

Perfect

Enchanted

Silent

Mysterious

Magnificent

Tranquil

Try using a place and an adjective together to create a new magical location. Here are some examples:

The Mystical Mountain

The Tranquil Temple

The Dazzling Desert

Can you write your own description of the place you have just invented?

Visit **nightzookeeper.com** to tell us all about the new magical location you have just imagined.

The Zoo Needs You!

Continue your adventure on
nightzookeeper.com

Create your own magical animals

Defeat
evil Voids

Rescue Sam the Spying Giraffe

Night Zookeeper uses storytelling
and technology to encourage creativity and
imagination. Our magical stories inspire
traditional creative play and develop reading,
writing, and drawing skills.

We believe in fairness and offer free
digital education products to all children
around the world.

Thank you for buying this book
and supporting our mission.

Visit **nightzookeeper.com**
for more information.

The adventure
continues in ...

NIGHT ZOO KEEPER

The Lioness of Fire Desert

Chapter One

Will Rivers, the Night Zookeeper, together with Riya, and Sam the Spying Giraffe, passed through the magical portal. Seconds before, they had said goodbye to the other giraffes and the lush coolness of the Whispering Woods. Now the three friends were standing in the fierce heat of the Fire Desert. Will felt his feet sinking into the fine sand. He could feel the warmth of it through his shoes. Sweat was already beading on his forehead.

'Wow, it's like stepping into an oven,' remarked Riya.

'Ouch, my hooves are burning,' grumbled Sam. 'Phff, phffff!' He lifted one front leg off the ground and blew on his hoof. Off-balance, the young giraffe wobbled and quickly shoved his hoof back down. Straight on top of Riya's foot.

'Ow!' she complained. 'Why are you so clumsy?'

Will was taking in their surroundings. They were encircled by sand, from low snaking ripples to towering dunes, stretching out endlessly in all directions. Surprisingly, they were also surrounded by water. Hundreds of silvery lakes, each reflecting the full moon, sat between the dunes. Many of the lakes were fringed by palm trees, but at the heart of each one was a swirling jet of flames as tall as a tree.

A recent memory blazed in Will's mind. The flames reminded him of the candles on his birthday cake. He thought for a moment. So much had happened since he had sneaked off from home: entering the Night Zoo; meeting Sam; being rescued by Riya; and helping to save the giraffes from those terrible Voids. And now, he was here, in the middle of this magnificent, forbidding desert with a job to do: he was the new Night Zookeeper. Except, he still didn't really know what that meant.

No-one had left any instructions. He took off his cap to wipe his forehead. He looked at the metal badge on the peak. It was the same shape as the purple elephant he had painted on the zoo wall and for some reason he thought of his Grandma Rivers. Will sighed. He suddenly really he missed her. He missed all his family, even his scruffy little brother. He missed home.

'What's up, Will?' asked Riya.

'Those flames. They look like the candles on my birthday cake,' said Will.

'Wow, must have been a big cake!' said Sam. Will smiled weakly and the giraffe continued, 'Hey, Riya, did you know I get heartburn every time I eat birthday cake?'

Riya shook her head. 'That's a shame,' she replied.

Sam gave her a goofy smile. 'Yeah, so the Doctor told me next time, take the candles off first!'

Riya rolled her eyes and groaned.

'What's the matter? You got a stomach-cake?' asked Sam. 'Geddit? Stomach-cake? Stomach-ache?'

'Argh, Will, can you make him stop?' said Riya.

'Sam, can you help?' asked Will. 'What can you see from up there?'

Sam raised his head as high as he could and peered around. 'Nothing really. Just sand and lakes and those twisty fiery thingies.'

Will turned to Riya. 'Which way do you think we should go? There are animals in trouble here, but I don't know where.'

Riya shrugged. 'Maybe you should try the Orb.'

'Wait a minute; there is something over there,' said Sam, squinting. 'It looks like . . . a big metal creature.'

A tingle of fear fizzed up Will's spine as recalled their recent battles in the Whispering Woods. 'Metal?' he repeated. 'It's not a Void, is it?'

'Not unless it's grown wings,' said Sam. 'And a moustache.'

'Huh?' said Will. 'What's it doing? Is it moving?'

'Not exactly. It's just sort of bobbing.'

'Bobbing?' replied Riya, baffled.

'Yes, on a lake. Oh, hang on. No, now it's twirling its moustache. Wow, look at it go.'

'Sam, are you feeling alright?' asked Will. 'You're not making much sense.'

'Oh, strange, it's stopped again,' noted Sam.

Riya suddenly put her face in her hands and groaned. Will looked alarmed. 'Riya? What's wrong?'

'I'm fine, I'm fine,' she replied with a wry smile. 'I know what it is. The metal creature.' She called up to Sam. 'Hey, Sam, have you never seen an aeroplane before? Or to be more precise, a seaplane?'

'What? Yes. I mean, of course I've seen a . . .

a plane before. Who hasn't?' he replied with a nervous laugh.

Riya looked at him suspiciously. 'Is that why you think its propeller is a moustache?' she scoffed.

'A plane!' exclaimed Will. 'Sam, pick me up so I can see, will you?'

Sam clamped his teeth on the collar of Will's coat and lifted him onto his back. Will grimaced as he felt warm dribble stream down the back of his neck. He wrapped his arms around the giraffe's neck to steady himself. Will stared out across the desert landscape. There was a flash of silver in the distance. There was a plane. An old silver seaplane was sitting next to the shore of a large lake.

Will felt hot breath on his ear. 'Will,' whispered Sam. 'Um, quick question.' The giraffe glanced down quickly at Riya.

'Yes?' Will whispered back.

'Will, what's a plane?' asked the giraffe.

Will smiled. 'I'd guessed you didn't know,' he replied under his breath.

'I've never left the Whispering Woods before,' explained Sam, sounding a bit embarrassed.

'It's alright,' Will said. 'What's a plane? Well, that's a plane and it might just be our ticket out of here. You were right, Riya. It's an old seaplane.'

Riya nodded with satisfaction. 'Knew it!'

Will suddenly noticed the plane's propeller

jerk and begin to rotate slowly. Thick smoke belched out of the sides of the nose. The whole plane shuddered as the propeller whirled up to speed. Seconds later, however, the engine spluttered to a halt again.

'No!' Will exclaimed. 'The moustache—I mean the propeller—is turning. Someone's trying to start the engine. We need to get down there before they leave!'

At that moment, there was a painfully loud screech of metal behind them. Sam was startled and Will toppled from his perch. He landed on his hands and knees in the soft sand. His heart was already pumping in his chest. Although he couldn't see the danger yet, he had heard that terrible sound before. He whipped off his backpack and drew out his torch.

The skyline at the top of the dune glowed red and then a grey metal head appeared. Will gasped as the robot spider crested the top of the dune in all its sleek, menacing glory.

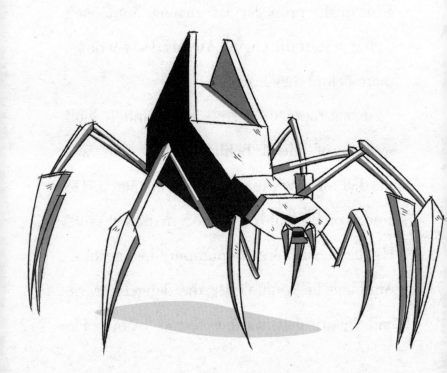

This Void was bigger, much bigger than the ones they had defeated in the woods. The giant robot halted and fixed its crimson eye on Will. His hand shaking, Will lifted the torch to aim it at the Void.

'Let it have it!' cried Riya. 'The light will drive that monster away!'

Will gritted his teeth and held the switch down. The torch rattled in his grip and a brilliant beam of light burst across the dune straight at the metal spider. To Will's astonishment, the Void didn't flinch. There was a soft hiss and a feeble puff of smoke as light struck metal, but the Void ignored it. Instead, it narrowed its red eye and advanced.

'I don't understand,' said Will. 'The torch.

It's not working like before.' A pulse of fear raced along his limbs.

'Then we definitely need to get down there before that plane leaves!' said Riya.

'Run for it!' shouted Will.

Will, Sam and Riya charged down the slope of the dune, stumbling and slipping on the sand. Will's heart was racing and his lungs hungry for air.

He glanced over his shoulder. The Void was chasing them. Will couldn't believe the torch beam had not affected the giant robot. Fortunately, the Void also seemed to be struggling in the soft conditions: its long, pointy legs were sinking deep into the sand under its enormous weight.

'This way!' shouted Sam, keeping his eyes fixed on the large lake.

'Is the plane still there?' gasped Riya. 'It hasn't taken off yet, has it?'

'No, it's still there,' Sam replied and then added, 'Sorry, what do you mean? Taken off?'

'I thought you knew what a plane was!' replied Riya. 'What do you think the wings are for? It takes off. It flies. Up in the air. Where we're going to get away from that robot!'

Sam's dark eyes flew open. 'But I can't fly!' he protested. 'I'm scared of heights!'

'What kind of giraffe is scared of heights?' cried Riya in disbelief.

Will looked back again. He almost smiled as he noted that the Void was losing ground. It was hissing in frustration as it became bogged down. 'Please stop arguing and keep going,' Will urged the others.

A few minutes later, they rounded a dune and Will spotted the seaplane on the lake ahead of them. He could also make out a figure in the cockpit.

'My ossicones are tingling,' announced Sam. 'That Void must be catching up!'

'That doesn't make sense,' said Riya, looking back. 'We're getting further away.'

Will peered into the cockpit. There was definitely someone there. Someone wearing a pilot's cap! Will felt a rush of hope. 'There's a person inside! A pilot!' he shouted and waved his arms frantically. 'Hey! Hey! Pilot, help! Start the plane!'

Sam suddenly skidded to a halt. Will and Riya stopped and looked back at him. 'Sam! What are you doing? Come on. The Void's coming!' said Will.

Sam was staring at the cockpit of the plane. The colour had drained from his face and his eyes were bright and glistening. 'That's no person, Will,' the giraffe replied quietly.

Will swivelled round to look at the plane. 'That's why my ossicones were warning me.' The figure in the plane threw open the cockpit window and a golden-brown face emerged. 'That's a lioness!' exclaimed the giraffe.

From across the lake, Will heard a rumbling, angry roar. The lioness pilot was baring her huge canine teeth and shaking a clenched paw at them. She ducked her head back inside the cockpit and frantically fiddled with the controls. The propeller began to rotate in fits and starts and smoke belched from the engine exhausts.

'Look! She must have heard me,' said Will. 'Come on, Sam!'

Sam's legs were shaking violently. 'You want me to fly?' he said forlornly. 'In a metal bird?

With a lion?'

'No choice, Sam,' said Will firmly. 'But to be safe, you might want to use that invisibility trick of yours.' Sam nodded eagerly and closed his eyes in concentration. The outline of the young giraffe's body began to glow until suddenly he became transparent and disappeared from sight.

As they approached the seaplane, the lioness pilot stuck her head out of the window again and shook her paw. The engine was coughing and popping and Will could barely make out what she was shouting: 'Grrr, stay back! Keep away from my plane! Grrr!'

Will and Riya pulled up on the shore next to the plane. Invisible Sam stood a few paces behind them, still quivering. 'Please help us!' Will called out. 'We're being chased.' Will pointed back along the shore. At that very moment, the giant Void lumbered into view. Its red eye was glowing furiously.

The lioness pilot turned to face them. Will immediately noticed an old wound on her face: a deep scar as straight as a ruler ran across her wide nose and down her jowl. Will realised immediately that he had been wrong. She wasn't angry; her amber eyes were full of fear. 'Leave me alone!' the lioness said. 'Go somewhere else. Why did you lead it here?'

Riya pleaded, 'You're our only chance.'

The lioness was staring wide-eyed at the approaching Void. 'No, I can't help you. I've got to go,' she said softly.

Suddenly, Will felt himself being hoisted into the air by the scruff of the neck. Unseen by the lioness, Sam lifted Will directly onto the plane's wing.

The lioness swung round and roared, 'No! There isn't time.'

'Please let us in!' said Will, clambering forwards towards the cockpit. Behind him, Sam deposited Riya on the wing.

The lioness glanced at the two children and then at the Void and then threw her paws up in the air. 'Alright, alright, get in!' she growled. She reached over and threw open the cockpit door. Will and Riya slipped and slid across the smooth wing towards the inside of the seaplane.

Ready for more great stories?

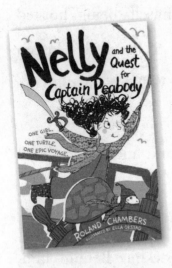